The King Next Do...

'And Jesus expected all those people to share your lunch? Silas, that is without doubt the biggest whopper you've ever told me. When are you going to stop making up these ridiculous stories?'

'But I'm not making it up this time, Mum. It's true! Jesus made it happen. I don't know how. Andrew says Jesus is a king. A king can do anything, can't he?'

In this new collection, ten familiar Bible stories are retold in the words of those who met Jesus for themselves.

Former actor Alan MacDonald now spends his time writing books, poems, radio and television drama. He lives in Nottingham, England, with his wife and three children.

For the children, young and old,
of St Paul's Church

The King Next Door

Alan MacDonald

Illustrations by Nick Ward

Text copyright © 1998 Alan MacDonald
Illustrations copyright © 1998 Nick Ward
This edition copyright © 1998 Lion Publishing

The moral rights of the author and artist
have been asserted

Published by
Lion Publishing plc
Sandy Lane West, Oxford, England
ISBN 0 7459 3897 3
Lion Publishing
4050 Lee Vance View, Colorado Springs,
CO 80918, USA
ISBN 0 7459 3897 3

First edition 1998
10 9 8 7 6 5 4 3 2 1 0

A catalogue record for this book is available
from the British Library

Library of Congress CIP data applied for

Printed and bound in Great Britain by Caledonian
International Book Manufacturing, Glasgow

Contents

Introduction

There are lots of books that tell stories about Jesus. This one is a bit different. These stories are told by the people who met Jesus and had their world turned upside down by him. Fishermen and servants, children and teachers —each of them saw a different view of Jesus and could tell a different tale. In this book, I've imagined how they might have told their stories in their own words. Most of the main characters actually appear in the Bible but sometimes I've given them imaginary names.

Each story adds another piece to our picture of Jesus, the king who lived next door. Jesus talked a lot about a kingdom. At the time I doubt if most people understood what he meant.

Some of them expected him to wear a crown and lead an army into war. But Jesus said his kingdom wasn't like that. It was already happening, right under people's noses— whenever someone loved and obeyed God. It could be seen most clearly of all in Jesus' own life. It was the kind of kingdom where children were welcomed, the sick were made well and no one was left outside God's love.

Today the kingdom is still growing—in the lives of Jesus' friends and followers all over the world.

Alan MacDonald

1

Jesus Goes Missing

Jerusalem was alive with noise and activity. It was the Passover festival and lots of visitors had come for the celebrations. The narrow streets were packed with people pouring in from the countryside. Street sellers in the markets called out to us to stop and buy. Smells of cooked meat, sweet perfumes, and fish piled high in baskets filled the air. I held on tightly to Jesus' arm to make sure we didn't lose him. He was twelve now. This was his first glimpse of the big city since the day he was blessed in the temple as a baby.

'Can we go and see the temple first, Dad?' he asked me eagerly.

I looked at my wife, Mary. 'Why not, Joseph?' she said. 'We can find a place to stay afterwards.'

As we entered the temple courtyard, Jesus stopped still. He gaped up at the white marble building, so tall it seemed to brush the clouds. The pillars, carved in gold, were as big as the trunks of cedar trees. In the afternoon sun the temple dazzled our eyes.

'Is it what you'd expected?' I asked Jesus.

He shook his head. 'Much, much better. No wonder they call it God's house.'

We took our lamb to be blessed by the priest for the Passover meal. Afterwards Jesus wanted to listen to the elders in the courtyard. He sat among the men as they talked about God and his laws.

'It's getting late,' said Mary at my side. 'We should find somewhere to stay before all the rooms are taken.'

I nodded. But Jesus didn't want to come away. He lingered on the steps, taking a last look back at the temple.

* * *

The week passed quickly. On the final day I met with friends from our village at the city gate. It was time to begin the long journey home. Mary had gone ahead with the other women from Nazareth. I meant to catch her up at the next stopping place. Jesus wasn't with me. I hadn't seen him since breakfast that morning. But I wasn't worried because I thought he'd gone ahead with his mother.

It was only when I saw Mary that evening that I realized I was wrong.

'Where's Jesus?' was the first thing she said to me.

I looked at her in surprise.

'What do you mean? He's with you.'

'No he isn't. I haven't seen him all day. I thought he was coming on with you and the other men.'

I felt the first stab of anxiety. If Jesus wasn't with Mary and he wasn't with me, where was he?

'He's probably with his friends,' I said. 'I saw Matthew and Daniel earlier. I'm sure he'll be with them.'

'I hope so,' said Mary with a worried frown. I could tell she blamed me for not taking better care of our son. We began to go round all our friends and relatives. No one had seen Jesus. Not even Matthew and Daniel. They said he hadn't turned up at the city gate that morning.

Mary bit her lip. 'We've left him behind,' she said. 'Our twelve-year-old boy. He's all alone in that great city back there.'

'He'll be all right.' I told her. 'He can look

after himself. It's too late to go back now. We'll have to set out tomorrow, as soon as it's light.'

'But why didn't he come with us?' Mary asked. 'He knew we were leaving today. Why would he have stayed behind?'

I couldn't answer that. I just prayed that wherever Jesus was, he was safe.

It took a whole day to retrace our steps to Jerusalem. Lamps were burning in the city when we arrived. It was no use searching in the dark. We found a room and tried to sleep. Most of the night we lay awake, thinking of our son, wondering where he was in the great city outside.

* * *

Early next morning we went to the market. None of the traders had seen a small, lost, dark-haired boy.

'Let's try the temple,' said Mary.

'Good idea. Remember how he didn't want to leave the first day we were there?' I replied.

That gave us hope. We climbed the hill to the temple, walking at first, then running when we were in sight of the walls.

Once in the courtyard we looked around. It was still busy, even though most visitors had gone home after the festival. I spotted a crowd of people under the shade of the arches. Some elders were talking to twenty or more people sitting at their feet. In the middle stood a dark-haired boy, who was the centre of attention.

The elders were asking him questions and marvelling at the boy's answers. It couldn't have been anyone else but Jesus.

We ran towards him. He smiled when he saw us coming, as if nothing was wrong. Mary wrapped him in her arms and hugged him over and over again.

'Where have you been? Where have you been?' she kept asking.

'Didn't you know we left two days ago?' I said angrily. 'Your mother and I have been out of our minds with worry.'

He looked at us in a puzzled way. 'Why were you worried? Didn't you know where I'd be?'

'How could we know that?' I asked.

'But it's where I belong. In my father's house.'

Mary and I didn't understand what he meant. We were just relieved and happy to have him back safe and sound.

* * *

Later, when he grew up, I often thought about that day. I'd been angry because I felt

Jesus' place was with me, at his father's side. But I was forgetting that Jesus' true Father was God. He was born to tell people about God's great love. So when he went missing, perhaps we should have known. Where else would he have been but in his Father's house?

2

Thirsty Work

I'm just a servant in this house. Servants have
to do everything.

'Jethro, fetch the water!'

'Jethro, make the fire!'

'Jethro, cook the dinner!'

At the end of the day I'm ready to crawl into
bed, I can tell you.

This week's been even busier than usual.
Luke got married. He's my master's only son
and a kinder boy you couldn't meet. Luke
married Esther, a girl from our village of Cana.
The two families have known each other for
years. All week we've been busy getting ready
for the wedding feast.

'Jethro, sweep the floor!'

'Jethro, run down to the market for some fruit!'

'Jethro, we need more oil for the lamps!'

I had to go backwards and forwards from morning till night.

My master and I argued about the wine. I said we needed more. He said we had plenty already. You can guess who won. I'm only a servant. Nobody listens to me.

* * *

On the night before the wedding, we all waited outside the house with our oil lamps burning in welcome. Luke had gone to bring Esther to her new home. We could hear the wedding procession coming, with drums and tambourines echoing down the street.

Luke and Esther were at the front. I think Luke was the proudest man in the world that night. And why shouldn't he have been—with a bride as lovely as Esther? I watched them enter the house, wiping a tear from my eye. But there was no time for crying—I had work to do. Tomorrow was the day of the wedding feast and everything had to be ready.

At noon the next day people started arriving. Everyone was invited. Uncles, aunts, cousins, great-grandmas and grandads. All the neighbours from our village came.

Mary from Nazareth arrived with her son, Jesus, and some of his friends. I'd heard a lot of stories about this Jesus. People said he was going to do great things. And they were right— as I found out.

The guests didn't go hungry. We'd made sure of that. There were bowls stacked high with bread. Fish as long as your arm. Grapes, figs, olives, nuts—there had to be plenty because a wedding feast goes on for days.

I was in charge of the wine. It was my job to make sure everyone had enough to drink.

My master stood up to wish the bride and bridegroom health and happiness. Then other people wanted to wish them God's blessing. Each time, everyone drank their wine. And each time I had to fill up their cups with more. I was starting to get worried. The wine was disappearing too fast. I tried to tell my master we needed more. But he waved me away: 'Not now Jethro, can't you see I'm talking?'

Nobody listens to me; I'm only a servant.

* * *

The next day my fears came true. I went to get another jar of wine and there was no more left. Not a drop. The other servants looked at me in dismay.

'What shall we do, Jethro?' they asked.

How was I to know? It was terrible. You can't have a wedding without anything to drink. The guests would be thirsty. My master would look a fool. Luke would feel ashamed. And I knew who would get the blame—Jethro!

One of the servants, a girl from Galilee, had an idea. 'Ask Jesus,' she said. 'You know how wise he is. Perhaps he'll know what to do.'

I didn't want to bother Jesus. He was busy talking. So I asked his mother, Mary, who was a friend of the family. By now every cup on the table was empty. No one had anything to drink. People were calling for me.

'Jethro, I'm thirsty!'

'Jethro, bring more wine!'

But I pretended not to hear. I hoped something would happen quickly.

By now Jesus had heard about our problem. He called me over and pointed to a corner.

'See those six big jars, Jethro? Go and fill them with water.'

Water? What good is that? I thought. But I did as he said. We took the jars to the well outside and filled them water. Then we carried them to Jesus. They were so heavy it took two of us to carry each jar.

'Now fill a cup and take it to the best man,' Jesus told me.

A cup of water for the best man? It was an insult! But I'm only a servant. Nobody listens to me.

The best man put the cup to his lips and tasted it. I waited for him to spit it out and start shouting at me. But instead a big smile spread over his face.

'What excellent wine!' he said. 'Most people

serve the best wine first but you've kept the best till now.'

I didn't know what to say. I was sure I'd given him a cup of water. But now it was a deep ruby red. The best wine you've ever tasted. I looked at Jesus. He raised his cup to me and laughed.

'Go on then, Jethro, people are waiting,' he said.

Everyone wanted to taste the new wine. I was kept busy filling their cups all day. But this time we didn't run out. Everyone ate and drank all they wanted. The guests laughed and talked until it was time to go to bed. It had been a day to remember. All thanks to Jesus. That was the day I realized he really was special. I'd never met anyone who could turn water into wine!

I was clearing the table when my master came back in.

He patted me on the back. 'You see, Jethro, admit I was right, wasn't I? We had plenty of wine to go round.'

I could have told him the truth. But I knew he'd never believe me. After all, I'm only a servant. Nobody listens to me!

3

Fish Aren't Stupid

Have you ever caught a fish? It's not as easy
as you might think. You have to know where
to fish, when to put your net down, and how
to pull it in slowly without breaking the net or
losing the fish. Fish aren't stupid. They don't
want to be caught and end up as someone's
dinner! They want to swim free and live a
long life. It takes a clever fisherman to catch
a fish.

I know all there is to know about fishing.
You ask anyone at the lake. Peter—he's the
man to ask for. I own a fishing boat with my
brother, Andrew. Sometimes we went out
fishing with our friends, James and John.

I was always the leader. It was me the others asked for advice.

'What shall we do then, Peter?'

'Row out further,' I'd say and we'd row out into deeper waters.

'Lower the nets,' I'd tell them, and the nets would go down into the shadowy green waters. We often came back with a good haul of fish. But the biggest catch we ever had? That was the day we went fishing with Jesus.

* * *

Andrew and I were sitting on the shore that day, mending our nets. We'd been out fishing all night and were tired. I glanced up from my work and saw Jesus standing over me. He was from Galilee like us, so I'd seen him before. I'd heard all the amazing stories about him, too.

'I'd like to borrow your boat,' he said, bold as you like.

'Why?' I asked. 'I didn't know you were a fisherman.'

'I don't want to fish,' he said. 'I need your

boat for something else. Can you push it out into the shallows?'

The truth was, I didn't much like lending our boat to anyone. But this wasn't just anyone asking—it was Jesus. So I jumped to my feet and did what he said.

When I got the boat into the water I realized a big crowd was watching me. Or rather, they were watching Jesus. Wherever he went hundreds of people always followed him. Now they were all waiting to see what he was going to do. Jesus got into the boat and Andrew and I pushed him out till the cool water was up to our waists. He told us that was far enough. Then he sat down in the boat and started to speak.

I saw now why he'd wanted my boat. His voice carried over the water as clear as music on a still night. Everyone could hear his words and they could see him plainly too. Andrew and I waded back to the shore and took up our nets again. But I listened as I worked. Jesus was saying that he had great news for us. That a new kingdom was coming and God would set people free. The weak, the blind, the old and the young—everyone could be part of this kingdom.

When he'd finished speaking, Andrew and I went to pull the boat back in.

'Wait. Why don't we go fishing?' said Jesus.

I stared at him. 'There's no point,' I said, shaking my head. 'We won't catch anything.'

Jesus raised his eyebrows. 'Why? Aren't there any fish left in the lake?'

I sighed. I really didn't want to explain but he gave me no choice. The truth was Andrew and I had been out all night. We had cast our nets in every one of our favourite spots but we hadn't caught a single fish. I explained this to Jesus wearily and waited for him to laugh. After all, wasn't I supposed to be one of the best fishermen in Galilee? What was the use of all my skill if I came home with an empty net?

Jesus waited until I'd finished. 'Row the boat out into deeper water,' he suggested. 'Then let's see what we catch.'

I shot a glance at Andrew. I didn't want to seem rude, but I knew a lot more about fishing than Jesus. If we hadn't been able to make a catch all night, there was no chance we were going to do better in broad daylight. Fish aren't stupid, as I've said.

Still, this was Jesus. I wasn't big-headed enough to give him a lecture, so we got into the boat with him.

I called to James and John on the shore. Then the five of us rowed out on the lake with our two boats side by side. After a while Jesus told us to stop.

'Let down the nets here,' he said.

'All right,' I said. 'But I warn you, we're wasting our time.'

We let the nets gently down into the water so they wouldn't make a big splash.

No sooner had we done so than I saw a fish. Then two, then three. Suddenly there were hundreds of them. They were jumping right into our net from all sides! When we tried to pull it in, the net was bursting with gleaming,

silver fish. I was afraid it would break with the weight of them.

'James! John!' I called, 'Give us a hand over here! Quickly!'

They brought their boat nearer and between us we managed to get the fish on board. There were so many that we filled the decks of both boats till they sank low in the water.

I turned to look at Jesus. He had made this happen. There was no other way to explain it. Fish aren't stupid. They don't normally go jumping into nets in broad daylight. For the first time I realized what kind of a king Jesus was. A king who could command the earth and sea, who could make even the fish obey him.

I fell on my knees before him in the boat. I don't mind telling you I was shaking.

'Lord, I'm not a good man. I'm not fit to be near you,' I gasped out.

Jesus lifted me to my feet. 'Don't be scared,' he said. 'These are only fish. Come with me and I'll teach you how to catch people for my Father's kingdom.'

We pulled the boats onto the shore. I looked at my nets, my boat and the huge catch of wriggling, silver fish. I could either carry on being a fisherman or follow Jesus. It didn't take me long to decide. As I said to Andrew, 'The fish aren't stupid—and nor am I. This kingdom of Jesus' is going to be worth seeing!'

4

A Hole in the Roof

Let me tell you about my friend Joshua.
Joshua hardly ever used to come out of his
house. If you passed by on the road, you'd see
him through the doorway. Most days he sat on
his bed all by himself. Joshua couldn't move
from the house. His poor, thin legs wouldn't
carry him. He hadn't been able to walk since
the day he was born. That was until something
changed his whole life. And all because of a
hole in a roof.

* * *

It all started the day I called round with
some exciting news.

'Joshua! It's me, Luke. Have you heard

who's at Eli's house?'

'How would I know?' asked Joshua. 'I don't hear anything stuck in here.'

He was sitting in the shadows staring out of the doorway as usual. I went and crouched down beside him.

'It's Jesus of Nazareth,' I said. 'Benjamin says he's the Messiah. The chosen King. We're

all going to Eli's house to see him. Why don't you come too?'

Joshua looked at me.

'How can I with these?' he said, pointing miserably at his thin legs. 'Don't make fun of me, Luke!'

'I'm not making fun,' I said. 'We could carry you. Benjamin and the others are waiting outside. We've got a mat for you to sit on. We're going to carry you through the town. Just like a great emperor!'

Joshua laughed at the idea. But he shook his head. 'No, you go without me. I'll only get in your way. Anyway what's the point in me being there?'

I squeezed his arm. 'Please, Joshua, come with us. I've heard wonderful stories about Jesus. He can make people better. Maybe he can do something about your poor legs. All we have to do is get you to see him.'

Joshua stared at the ground. 'I'll never walk, Luke. You know I won't,' he sighed.

But ten minutes later we were walking down

the road. Joshua was seated on the rush mat. We'd tied it to two poles so we could carry him between us. People stopped to stare as we went past.

'Clear the way! Clear the way for the Emperor Joshua!' I shouted in a loud voice. Benjamin and the others laughed. Even Joshua smiled. He wasn't used to people paying him attention.

Eli's house was the biggest in our village. He owned a vineyard and paid people to pick his grapes. Eli was very proud of his large house with the cleanly swept courtyard. But today even Eli's house wasn't big enough. Crowds of people filled the room and spilled out onto the street. Everyone in the village wanted to get a glimpse of Jesus.

We lowered Joshua to the ground and looked at the packed doorway hopelessly. Joshua could tell what I was thinking.

'It was a good idea, Luke, but we'll never get in. We can't even get near the door.'

Benjamin nodded his head sadly. 'He's right.

We can't carry Joshua through all those people. We may as well go home.'

I shook my head. We'd carried Joshua this far. I wasn't going to give up now. I was sure that if we could only get Joshua to see Jesus he would help. I looked at Eli's house. There were people thronging around the door and peering in the window holes. The only place that wasn't crowded was the roof.

'That's it!' I said out loud. 'The roof! We'll carry Joshua up onto the roof!'

Benjamin looked at me as if I was crazy. 'What good will that do? Jesus is inside. How are we going to get him to come up to the roof?'

'We won't have to,' I replied. 'We'll lower Joshua down to see Jesus.'

The others were still looking at me as if I'd lost my mind.

'Think!' I said. 'The roof is only made of mud and sticks. So all we've got to do is make a hole in it. Then we can lower Joshua down to Jesus.'

Joshua glanced up at me with a worried expression.

'Lower me down? You're joking, aren't you, Luke?'

'Don't worry, Joshua,' I grinned. 'We won't drop you.'

Steps at the side of Eli's house led up to the roof. It wasn't easy getting Joshua up them. But we finally made it and set him down safely onto the flat top of the house.

'Let's get digging,' I said.

'Eli's not going to like it,' frowned Benjamin. 'It's his roof.'

'It's an emergency,' I argued. 'Joshua has *got* to see Jesus. He'll never get another chance like this.'

So we started digging. It was hot work under the midday sun but soon we'd made a little hole in the roof. We began to make it wider with our hands. Soon I could see an angry face staring up at us from below.

'Hey! What's going on up there? Look what you've done to my roof!'

It was Eli. He wasn't at all pleased. But we couldn't help that.

Slowly we started to lower Joshua down through the hole. Hands reached up from below to support him. At last he was safely on the ground. Jesus looked up at us through the hole.

'You must care about your friend very much,' he said. I watched him bend down to Joshua and take his hand.

'Joshua, you are forgiven,' he said kindly.

Some of the teachers from our local temple were sitting nearby. I saw their faces darken. Jesus was forgiving Joshua for all the wrong things he'd ever done. But no one could forgive except God himself! The teachers were furious at what Jesus had just said.

Jesus guessed what they were thinking. 'Which is easier?' he asked. 'To say to this boy, "You are forgiven," or to say, "Get up and walk?"' Nobody answered. A hush had now fallen in the house. Every eye was on Jesus. The whole village knew that Joshua had never been able to walk. Could Jesus really change that? I lay on my stomach, watching through the hole, hardly daring to move.

Jesus turned to the crowd and said, 'So that you know I can forgive—Joshua, pick up your mat and go home.'

Joshua sat up and took Jesus' hand. He rose

slowly but steadily to his feet. Then he walked
to the door, the crowd parting to let him
through.

I stared after him in amazement. I had
heard all kinds of wonderful stories about Jesus.
Now I knew they were all true. A king was
living among us in Galilee. A king who could
make the impossible happen.

For the next week people in our village
talked about nothing else except the miracle.
Joshua had a constant stream of visitors at his
house. They wanted to see him walking with
their own eyes. One of them was Eli.

'Hello,' said Joshua. 'As you can see, I'm still
walking.'

'Good,' said Eli. 'Then you and your friends
can walk straight round to my house. I'm still
waiting for someone to mend the hole in my
roof!'

5

The Whopper Picnic

Silas doesn't lie exactly. He just tells what I call
'whoppers'. Half of what he says is true and
the other half is made up. The trouble is his
tongue just runs away with him. He can't help
himself. He just keeps talking and talking until
the story has turned into one of his whoppers.
You know it's nonsense because the things Silas
tells you are crazy—like the time he said he'd
seen a camel with three humps.

I just laugh when Silas says things like that.
I'm his mother and I hear them every day. So
when he told me about Jesus I didn't believe
him at first.

* * *

'He's amazing,' said Silas. 'Once, he put mud on the eyes of a blind man. And when the mud was washed off the blind man could see.'

'Is that one of your whoppers, Silas?' I asked.

'No, it's the honest truth. Grandma told me.' Grandma doesn't usually tell whoppers. So that one had me puzzled.

Silas wanted to go and see Jesus. He said that all his friends were going. They'd seen Jesus coming across the lake in a boat.

'Please can I go? Please, Mum! If I run now, I'll get there before him,' he chattered.

I made Silas wait while I packed him some food. I wasn't having him go off for the afternoon without anything to eat. Silas kept

running in and out impatiently.

'Come on, Mum, I'll be too late,' he complained.

I wrapped up five brown rolls and two small fish in a cloth and gave them to him.

'Here, take these. And make sure you remember to eat them,' I said. (He's always forgetting to eat.) Silas grabbed the food and ran off towards the lake.

He was gone all day. It was getting dark when he arrived back. I was beginning to worry about him. The moment he got in the door he started babbling with excitement.

'Sorry I'm late. It took me hours to get home. I couldn't help it. Wait till I tell you about Jesus…'

'Oh, you did see him, then?' I said.

'See him? Better than that, I spoke to him! And I helped him do the most amazing thing. You won't believe it, Mum.'

I narrowed my eyes. 'Silas, if this is going to be one of your whoppers, I don't want to hear it.'

'It's true, Mum. On my life.'

'Go on then,' I sighed. When Silas has got a story to tell it's no use trying to stop him.

'Well, there were lots of us who went to hear Jesus. A massive great crowd. Thousands. Probably millions,' He caught my eye. 'Well, a lot anyway.'

I raised one eyebrow.

'Jesus stood on a big rock where we could all see him,' continued Silas. 'I was at the front, really close to him. I could hear every word he said. He told us stories. There was one about a shepherd who goes searching for one silly sheep that gets lost.'

'Stories, eh? That's something you know all about, Silas,' I said. 'Did you eat your lunch, by the way?'

'That's the amazing bit,' said Silas. 'It was getting late and lots of people had come without anything to eat…'

'I don't find that amazing,' I remarked. 'Most people have got no more sense than silly sheep.'

'Yes,' said Silas. 'But Jesus' friends wanted to send us all home. So we could buy something to eat in the villages. And I heard Jesus arguing with them. He said, "Why don't *you* give them something to eat?"'

'What? Thousands of them? And how could they do that?'

'Wait till you hear the next bit,' Silas said. 'One of Jesus friends—his name was Andrew—asked if anyone had any food. So I showed him my lunch.'

'That was a daft thing to do,' I said. 'I suppose he wanted some himself.'

'Well no, not exactly. He took me to see Jesus and I showed him my rolls and fish. Jesus asked if I would share them.'

'Share them?' I made a tutting noise. Silas went on quickly.

'Anyway, when he'd asked God to bless the food, Jesus told everyone to sit down in groups. Then he asked Andrew and the others to share the food out among them.'

'Hold on. What food?'

'My lunch.'

At this point I burst out laughing. I couldn't help it. 'But you said there were *thousands* of people, Silas.'

'Yes.'

'And Jesus expected them all to share five rolls and two fish?'

'Yes,' repeated Silas, earnestly.

'Silas! Go on, admit it. You're making all this up.'

'I'm not! I haven't finished yet, Mum. Listen. Andrew and the others started to give out the bread and fish. They gave some to each group. And when they'd given it out Jesus always seemed to have more. Until in the end everyone had something to eat.'

'You mean he found some extra food from somewhere?'

'No. I told you, Mum, it was just my five rolls and two fish. That's all there was. Honest. And this is the really amazing bit. When we'd all finished eating I helped Andrew clear up. And we filled twelve baskets with the left-over pieces! Twelve! Isn't that incredible?'

He finally stopped chattering. I sat back and shook my head at him.

'Silas, that is without doubt the biggest whopper you've ever told me. When are you going to stop making up these ridiculous stories?'

'But I'm not making it up this time, Mum. It's true!'

'How can it be true?' I said, 'It's impossible!'

'Jesus made it happen. I don't know how. Andrew says Jesus is a king. A king can do anything, can't he?'

Nothing I said would make Silas admit he was lying. In the end I ruffled his hair and told him to go to bed. 'It's a good story, my boy. You believe it if you want to.'

Silas sighed heavily.

'Are you going to help me then?' he asked.

'Help you do what?'

'Get the basket in from outside.'

'What basket? What are you talking about?'

'The one Andrew let me keep. It's full of the bread and fish we didn't eat. It took me hours to drag it home. That's why I was so late.'

I went outside to look, not expecting to see anything. But there in the pale moonlight was a basket. It was full to the brim with fish and rolls. Enough food to feed our whole family for a week.

I looked at the basket, then at Silas. For once I couldn't think of a single word to say. Silas had been telling the truth after all. It wasn't one of his whoppers. The only whopper was the basket of food we dragged into the house that night!

6

Two Silver Coins

I'm Solomon. I teach people God's laws. I'm an expert; I know what is right and what is wrong. So when I met Jesus I wanted to test him out.

'Teacher,' I said. 'What must I do to live for ever?'

'You're the expert,' he replied. 'What does it say in the Scriptures?'

I knew the answer to that one. 'Love God with all my heart and love other people just like I love myself.'

'True,' said Jesus. 'Do that and you will live.'

He wasn't going to shut me up that easily. I wanted to show him that I was clever too.

'But who are the people I should love?' I asked.

Jesus looked at me. Then, to my surprise, he started to tell a story. I listened, along with the rest of the crowd that had gathered.

* * *

'Once, a man set out on a journey,' Jesus said. 'He was going from Jerusalem down to Jericho. It was a long journey through rocky hill country. So he took money, clothes, food and water and loaded them onto his donkey.

'The sun beat down as the traveller turned a bend in the road. There were tall rocks on either side, casting long shadows. This part of the journey was dangerous. Robbers lived in the hills. Sometimes they came down from the caves where they lived and lay in wait on the road.

'The traveller looked around him anxiously. He urged his donkey to walk faster. Then, without warning, a band of robbers jumped out on him. There were three of them and there was nothing he could do. They pulled the traveller off his donkey and beat him with clubs. Stripping off his clothes, they stole his donkey and everything he had. The wounded man heard them running off down the road. But he was too badly hurt to get up.

'He lay there for what seemed an age, with the sun scorching his bare back. At last he heard footsteps coming up the road. Fearing the robbers had come back, the man lifted his head. It wasn't the robbers; it was a priest on his way from Jerusalem. Priests served God in the temple. Surely this one would stop and help?

'The priest saw the man in the road, bleeding and helpless. He paused. Then he walked quickly past, afraid the robbers might still be lurking nearby.

'The man groaned and lay back. His throat was dry and his head throbbed. Soon he heard someone else coming. Turning his head, he croaked out, "Help! Please, help me!"

'This time it was a Levite. Levites helped the priests with their duties in the temple. *He is bound to stop*, thought the man. The Levite bent over to look at him. Then he glanced around anxiously, and hurried on his way.

'The sun began to sink behind the hills. The man thought he would lie on that road for ever. He thought about his wife and children and wondered if he would ever see them again.

'Finally, someone else came along. A Samaritan. *Just my luck!* thought the man. Jews and Samaritans hated each other—and he was a Jew. A Samaritan would be the last person to help him.

'To his surprise, he heard the stranger stop his donkey.

'"Heavens! What happened to you? Let me help," said the Samaritan. He took a water skin from his own donkey and gave the man a drink. Then he tore up his own shirt and used it to clean the man's wounds with oil and wine.

'Soon the man was sitting on the Samaritan's donkey, leaning heavily on his companion.

'A few miles down the road, they came to an inn. The Samaritan lifted the man from his

donkey and carried him inside to a comfortable bed.

"How can I thank you?" asked the man in a weak voice. "If you hadn't helped me, I might have died."

"Rest and get better," said the Samaritan. 'I've told the innkeeper to take care of you."

'The man looked worried. "But I haven't any money to pay him. The robbers took it all."

'"Don't worry," said his new friend, "I've paid him two silver coins. If he spends any more, I've told him I will pay. I'll come back on my way home and see how you are. Now rest."

'The man lay back on his pillow. He couldn't think of the words to thank this kind stranger who had saved his life.'

* * *

Jesus paused. His story was finished but now he had a question for me.

'Which of the three men showed love to the man who was robbed?' he asked.

How would you have answered? The priest should have helped one of his own people, but he didn't. Neither did the Levite. Only the Samaritan, a stranger from another country, showed kindness.

'The one who took care of him,' I answered.

Jesus smiled and nodded. 'You go and do the same.'

I went away, thoughtfully. I had wanted to catch Jesus out, but instead his story had set me thinking. Maybe I wasn't always right. In the past I had regarded Samaritans as worse than dogs. But Jesus's story had made me wonder if God loved them the same as me.

A beggar was sitting by the road, holding out his hand. I'd passed him on that road many times before. Most days I never gave him a second look. But if Samaritans were God's children, perhaps beggars were too.

I went over to the beggar and took out some money. Putting the coins in his dirty hand, I told him to buy some food. The beggar stared at the money I'd given him. Two shining silver coins. It was a lot of money, but no more than the Samaritan had given.

7

My Lazy Sister

Aren't sisters a pain? At least, my sister is.
Maybe you've got a sister who makes your
bed, tidies your room and makes your
breakfast every morning. My sister Mary
isn't a bit like that. The two of us are always
arguing.

People often say, 'Mary and Martha are
so alike, aren't they?' But we're not really.
I'm quick at things; Mary is slow. I like to sit
quietly and do my sewing; Mary likes singing.
I wake up early; Mary stays in bed dreaming.
Most of the time we get on all right. But
sometimes Mary drives me up the wall. Like
one time that Jesus came to see us. That was

the day I really lost my temper with my lazy
sister.

* * *

Jesus' visits were always a surprise. We live
in Bethany, a little village near Jerusalem. So
whenever our friend Jesus went to Jerusalem he
came to stay with Mary, me and our brother
Lazarus. We loved seeing him. Whenever we
saw him on the road we'd all drop what we
were doing and run to meet him.

Sometimes he would stay the night at our
house. His friends—Peter, Andrew, James and
John—often came too. They were fishermen
with loud voices and strong opinions. Then the
house would ring with talk and laughter late
into the evening.

One morning I was sweeping the courtyard
outside. Mary was out for a walk somewhere.
She often goes off on her own, humming a
tune to herself. Of course, she never thinks
to ask if I need any help first. While I was
sweeping I heard a voice call my name. I
looked up to see Jesus with Peter and the others.

They were on their way to Jerusalem. I welcomed them and ran to call Lazarus.

I was always glad to see Jesus, but today it put me in a fluster. There were five hungry guests and we didn't have a meal ready. Guess who'd have to do the cooking? Mary was out, so it was all up to me as usual! I started to think. I'd have to bake fresh bread and fetch water from the well. There was a lot to do.

A little later Mary drifted in. By this time I was getting hot and bothered.

'Where have you been?' I demanded.

'Just out for a walk,' she said. 'Why? What's the matter?'

'Oh, nothing. Jesus is here, that's all.'

'Jesus?' said Mary, her face lighting up.

'Yes, with Peter and the others. They'll all be waiting for a meal but... Mary, come back!'

Mary hadn't stayed to listen. She'd heard the name Jesus and rushed straight inside. I sighed heavily. Maybe when she'd said hello she would come back to help me. But ten minutes later she still hadn't returned.

I trudged off to the well to fetch some water. Jesus and his friends would be hot and dusty from the road. They'd want to wash their hands and feet.

After I'd fetched the water, I lit the fire in the clay oven. As I watched the dry grass burn I was getting more and more cross with Mary. Why should I be out in the courtyard doing all the work while she sat talking to Jesus? It wasn't fair. I had a good mind to go in, grab her by the arm and drag her outside.

When the bread was baked I took it in. Everyone took some of the flat bread to eat.

I'd warmed a bowl of lentils too. Jesus dipped his bread in and scooped some up. He smiled at me. 'Thank you, Martha. Why don't you sit down to eat with us?'

I shook my head. There was still work to do.

I looked pointedly at Mary. She could at least come and help now. I'd done most of the hard work. But my lazy sister didn't even look up! Jesus had started telling another story and Mary was hanging on his every word. She ate her bread without even thinking who'd baked it. I felt like giving her a good kick. Nobody even noticed me!

The next time I came in, with a jar of wine, Mary was talking to Jesus.

'But why?' she was asking. 'Why go to Jerusalem again, Jesus? You know that the teachers of the law hate you. It's dangerous in the city.'

Jesus started to answer. But I wasn't listening. I was watching my lazy sister. I stood there with the wine jar in my hand, waiting to catch her eye. At last I lost patience and pushed a cup in front of her face.

'Do *you* want some wine, Mary?' I said coldly.

She took the cup without even looking at me. 'Oh thanks, Martha.'

That was it! I lost my temper and slammed the cup down beside her. It broke in pieces. Mary nearly jumped out of her skin.

'What did you do that for?' she asked in surprise.

I turned to Jesus. At least he would understand.

'Tell her please, Master,' I said. 'Tell my lazy, idle sister.'

'What do you want me to tell her?' asked Jesus. He was looking at me with concern.

'To come and help me!' I said. 'Ever since you got here she hasn't lifted a finger. It's been left to me to fetch and carry and cook and serve. I haven't stopped for the last hour!'

'I've noticed,' said Jesus.

'Well? Don't you care?' I said, almost crying with rage. 'Is it fair that I do all the work and my sister does nothing?'

I waited for Jesus to turn on Mary. I wanted him to tell her off in front of everyone. To make her look small and stupid. But he didn't. He took my hand and made me sit down next to him.

'Martha,' he said softly. 'Why are you so

upset? There's no need to wear yourself out making a big feast for us. Food and drink aren't important. What matters is that you're hungry to know God.'

I couldn't believe my ears. Was Jesus taking Mary's side instead of mine?

'You want me to send Mary away?' he asked. I sniffed and nodded.

'But that wouldn't be right. Mary is eager to learn. I won't be with you for ever. Why don't you stay and talk to me too?'

So I stayed and talked with Jesus. And slowly I started to calm down inside. I was still angry with Mary but I began to see what Jesus meant. By going to so much trouble over the meal I was missing the best part. Being with Jesus was far more important than cooking. After all, if a king came to your house, you'd be silly to stay in the kitchen the whole time!

So Jesus talked and I asked questions. In fact, I got so caught up talking that I didn't notice the time. When Jesus got up to go I realized I hadn't moved for hours.

I rose to clear away the bowls from the meal. But someone had already done it. I looked up and saw Mary smiling at me. She'd cleared away quietly, so that I could carry on listening. Perhaps my lazy sister isn't all bad after all.

8

Climbing Trees

I'm married to Zacchaeus. You might have heard of him. He's a very important man, my husband. He's in charge of collecting all the taxes in our city of Jericho. It's a big city—Jericho. Lots of rich, important people live here. And they all have to pay their tax money to my husband. Of course, sometimes he used to charge a bit extra. A coin here, a coin there. Who was to know he was cheating people? It made us rich. We used to live in a fine, big house with lots of servants. We even had our own well in the courtyard.

We don't live there any more, though. Last month we moved into a smaller house. And all

because my fool of a husband climbed a tree.
You don't believe me? Let me tell you the
story.

***

One day Zacchaeus came home all of a
dither. I was just getting ready for the visitors
I was expecting.

'Hannah! He's coming!' cried Zacchaeus.
'Have you heard? He could be here any
minute.' He was dancing about in the doorway
as if someone was tickling his toes.

'What are you talking about?' I said, 'I'm
busy. I've got guests coming for lunch.'

'Never mind them,' said Zacchaeus. 'It's that
man everyone's talking about—Jesus. They say
he's a king, the one God's chosen to save us.'

'Oh him. Who cares about him?' I said.
We get all kinds of crackpots in a city like
Jericho. Magicians, healers, fortune-tellers—
I've seen them all before. But Zacchaeus was
convinced this Jesus was different. Someone
special.

'I want to see him,' he said. 'It's not often we

get to see a king in our city. Are you coming or not?'

'No I am not,' I told him. 'Do you think I'm going to stand on the street with beggars and poor people?'

The truth is that I don't like going out much. Sometimes I get called names in the street. Like 'greedy pig', 'bloodsucker' and 'money-grubber'. It's because of Zacchaeus' job. Everyone hates tax collectors. They take people's money and give it to the Roman government.

But Zacchaeus didn't care if people called him names. He had set his heart on seeing Jesus. So I said, 'You go, then. Just keep out of trouble, that's all.'

I waited for my visitors to arrive for lunch. I waited and waited. Nobody came. The food was going cold.

At last I went down to the main street to see what was going on.

When I got there, I could hardly believe my eyes. It looked as if the whole city had turned out to see Jesus. The main road though Jericho is lined with trees. Beneath the trees crowds pressed forward on every side. No wonder my visitors hadn't arrived. They'd come to see Jesus like everyone else.

I looked around but I couldn't see Zacchaeus anywhere. My view was blocked by some idiot's feet hanging down. He was sitting on the branch of a tree above my head. Can you imagine it? A grown man climbing a tree!

I wasn't the only one staring up at him. Lots of people were. Because the man called Jesus had stopped in the middle of the road. He was talking to the fool up the tree.

Just then the fool looked down and I saw his face. What a shock I got. It was my own husband!

'ZACCHAEUS!' I screamed.

'Oh Hannah, there you are!' he smiled. 'Wonderful news! You won't believe it!'

'You're up a tree!' I said.

'Well, yes,' he replied. 'I was too short to see over the crowds from down there.'

'But a tree!' I hissed. 'People will think you've
gone mad! They're laughing at you.'

I can't tell you how silly I felt talking to my

husband up a tree. I'd gone quite red in the face. I could feel every pair of eyes staring at us. But Zacchaeus didn't seem to mind a bit. He was too excited.

'Wait till you hear what Jesus said. We've got to hurry. He wants to come to our house.'

'To our house?' I said.

'Yes!' And before I knew it Zacchaeus had shinned down the tree and was dragging me home by the hand.

Well, Jesus did come to our house. And you should have seen the jealous looks on our neighbour's faces. As I told you, they've never liked us. 'Fancy going to the house of a man like that!' they whispered. 'A greedy, grasping tax collector. Doesn't Jesus know who he is?'

I'll say this for Jesus. He didn't seem to care whether we were princes or beggars. He sat down at our table and ate the food I brought. And then he started talking. I could see Zacchaeus hanging on his every word. As if this was the day he'd been waiting for all his life.

Jesus stayed a long time at our house. Over two hours (I made sure the neighbours heard about that).

When he'd gone, Zacchaeus started acting very oddly. He went round the house collecting things in a box. Rugs, candlesticks, pots, bread and olives...

'Where do you think you're taking those?' I asked.

'To the poor people,' he replied.

'Are you mad? Those are our things! They belong to us!' I said.

He kissed me on the forehead. 'Hannah, dearest. Jesus helped me understand. God loves me. ME! Zacchaeus. And so we don't need all these things. We can use them to help other people and show our love for God.'

I couldn't believe my ears. Zacchaeus had never talked this way before. Perhaps he'd bumped his head when he was climbing that tree.

'Are you feeling all right?' I asked.

He beamed at me. 'I've never felt better in

my life. You'll see, Hannah. Our lives are going to change.'

And he was right. Our lives did change. We got poorer and everyone else got richer! Every week Zacchaeus kept giving things away. And he paid back everyone he'd cheated in the past.

Soon we moved to a smaller house and had to pay off the servants. But here's the funny thing: the poorer we get the happier Zacchaeus seems to be. I can't understand it. He says that we're worth more to God than all the money in the world.

Maybe one day, when nobody's looking, I'll climb a tree myself and see what happens. But don't tell anyone I said so.

9

The King's Donkey

My name's Ruth—and Dusty is my donkey.
He's only a colt really—a young donkey—but
he once carried a king on his back. I'll never
forget the day it happened.

* * *

I was feeding Dusty his lunch when two men
came to our door. It wasn't a surprise to see
visitors. Lots of people pass through our village
on the road to Jerusalem. From our house you
can see the temple roof high above the great
city. On a hot day travellers sometimes stop
to ask for a drink. Especially at Passover time,
when thousands of visitors flock to the city for
the festival. It's the busiest time of the year.

The two men weren't thirsty. They were
looking at Dusty.

'Is that your young donkey?' one of them
asked.

'Yes,' I said. 'Do you want to stroke him?'

They came over and patted Dusty's neck.
He likes people and he was soon nuzzling their
hands and eating the grass they offered him.

I went to get my mum. She likes me to tell
her if someone comes to the door.

'Can I help you?' she asked.

'I hope so. We'd like to borrow your young donkey,' said one of the men. He smiled in a friendly way.

'Dusty?' said Mum. 'What do you want him for?'

'Our master would like to ride him,' said the man. 'Have you heard of Jesus from Galilee?'

Mum and I looked at each other. Had we heard of Jesus? We'd heard of no one else for the past week. Recently a near neighbour of ours had died. His name was Lazarus and he lived with his sisters, Mary and Martha. We were all very upset until we heard Jesus had been to see them. Jesus brought Lazarus back to life! The news spread like wildfire through all the villages. People wanted to know all about Jesus. When was he coming? Was he the king promised to our people? Would he lead an army against the hated Romans who ruled us?

I couldn't think what a king would want with a donkey like Dusty. Surely a king would ride on a horse or in a golden chariot?

'No one's ever ridden Dusty before,' I said.

'Then Jesus will be the first,' smiled the man. 'Don't worry, we'll bring him back safely.'

In the end Mum and I agreed. For one thing we were curious to see Jesus for ourselves. And if we let him borrow Dusty, we had an excuse to go along too.

Jesus was waiting for us on the hill called the Mount of Olives. There was a large crowd with him already. Everyone had heard he was on his way to Jerusalem. They wanted to see if the king was going to claim his throne at last. Some of Jesus' friends arranged their cloaks on Dusty's back to make a rough saddle. Then Jesus patted his neck gently and climbed on his back.

Mum and I exchanged worried glances. I'd only once ever tried to ride on Dusty's back. He'd kicked and bucked so much that I fell off in no time. But Dusty stood quietly while Jesus got on. Then he ambled slowly off along the road. You would have thought he was born to carry a king.

As we left the olive groves and climbed the

steep hill towards the city gate, the crowd around us started to grow. I'd never seen so many people. Visitors were pouring into Jerusalem from every direction. When they saw Jesus they gladly joined our procession.

Mum and I walked just behind Dusty with Jesus' friends. Everyone was talking excitedly. Someone climbed a palm tree, stripped off some branches and threw them down to us. We picked them up and began to wave them like royal banners. People standing at the roadside cheered. Some of them threw their cloaks on the road for Jesus to pass over. I had never felt so proud in my life. I wanted to tell them all that it was my donkey Jesus was sitting on.

One of Jesus' friends shouted:

'God bless the king! The king who comes in the name of the Lord!'

Other voices took up the cry and soon the shouts rang out all along the road.

'The king is coming! Blessed is the kingdom of our father David!'

Children were waving at Jesus. The cheers echoed to the walls of Jerusalem. Some ran ahead on the road, telling everyone that Jesus was coming. Jesus himself sat on Dusty, nodding and smiling to the crowd as he rode past. He wasn't at all how I'd imagined a king. Children came and ran alongside him and he seemed pleased to see them.

But not everyone was pleased to welcome

Jesus to Jerusalem. Ahead of us a circle of grim-faced men waited under a tree. They were teachers of the law, men who made up hundreds of rules for people to keep. My grandma said the temple teachers hated Jesus because people listened to him rather than obeying their rules.

One of the teachers stepped out in the road in front of us.

'God bless the king!' shouted voices all around us.

The man in the road glared and pointed at Jesus.

'Tell your followers to be quiet!' he thundered.

Jesus shook his head. 'If they were quiet, the stones on the road would cry out!' he answered.

He rode on up the hill. As we passed the teachers of the law I heard them muttering dark threats. They were plotting to get rid of Jesus. (At the time I was too excited to pay much attention. Only afterwards, when Jesus was arrested, I remembered what they'd said.)

Nothing could spoil that day. The day when I walked behind a king. When the whole of Jerusalem seemed to be singing with hope and excitement. The day when Dusty carried Jesus through the cheering crowds. I still didn't understand why Jesus had chosen a poor little donkey to ride. But my grandma knew. When I got home and told her the whole story, she nodded her head.

'Just as it's written. Just as the prophet Zechariah said it would happen, hundreds of years ago,' she said.

'What, Grandma?' I asked. 'What is written?'

Grandma could remember it word for word:

'Shout for joy, people of Jerusalem,
Look, your king is coming to you!
He comes in triumph and victory
But gentle and riding on a donkey,
on a colt, the young of a donkey.'

She explained that by riding Dusty, Jesus was telling everyone that he *was* the promised king. Not a king in a chariot at the head of a great army, but a king riding on a humble donkey. A king who came in peace, without drums or trumpets or swords—bringing only the message of God's great love.

10

The Stranger on the Road

My name is Cleopas. I was one of the many who followed Jesus. I saw him arrested and put to death in Jerusalem.

A few days after he died I decided to return to my home. Emmaus is a little village about eight miles outside Jerusalem. My friend Levi came to keep me company on the road. We trudged along in low spirits, talking about the things we'd seen over the past days.

'I feel like my life has ended,' I said to Levi. 'Without Jesus I don't know what I'm going to do.'

Levi nodded his head sadly. He felt the same way. Ever since we'd met Jesus, life had been

filled with exciting discoveries. Now it seemed
dull and empty, hardly worth getting up for in
the morning.

We were so lost in gloom that we didn't
notice a stranger on the same road as us. He
caught up and walked alongside us. I didn't
pay him much attention. All I remember is
that he had a brown cloak wrapped around
him.

'You both seem rather sad,' he remarked. 'Is there anything the matter?'

We stopped in the road and looked at him in surprise.

'Are you the only visitor to Jerusalem who hasn't heard what's happened?' I said.

He shrugged.

'You must have heard of Jesus of Nazareth, surely?' Levi said.

'I've been away. Tell me about him,' he replied.

So we began to tell the story of Jesus from the beginning. It was a relief to talk about how we were feeling. And the stranger had a way of listening that drew the story out of us.

'I thought Jesus was the king promised to Israel. The true Messiah,' I began. 'I'd never met anyone like him before. I followed him to Jerusalem. I was there among the cheering crowd that welcomed him to the city. *Now he'll claim his crown*, I thought. *This is where it all starts to happen.* But I was wrong. That was the day it all started to go wrong.'

Levi took over the story. He explained how the teachers of the law hated Jesus. How they had him arrested, told lies about him and put him on trial. He described how we'd watched Jesus hang on a cross and die like a criminal.

'So you see,' I ended up. 'Jesus is dead and all our hopes have come to nothing. We have no king to follow any more. They buried him three days ago.'

'But that isn't all,' added Levi. 'Early this morning some of our women went to Jesus' grave. They came running back saying it was empty and the body had gone.'

I gave a hollow laugh. 'They claimed to have seen angels who said that Jesus was alive.'

This time it was the stranger's turn to stop in the road and look at us.

'Alive?' he repeated.

'Yes, the women are upset, of course. They're imagining things.'

The stranger shook his head slowly. 'But how can you be so foolish? So slow to believe?'

Levi and I glanced at each other. One

minute our companion said he didn't know anything about Jesus and the next he was calling us fools!

'What do you mean?' I said angrily. 'You'd better explain or you can walk by yourself!'

So the stranger began to talk. He explained to us what was written in the Scriptures about Jesus. He reminded us that long ago the prophet Isaiah had predicted a suffering servant would come. One who would be led away like a lamb to be killed. A king who would be put to death to save his people.

Levi and I listened without a word. We were amazed. Only Jesus had ever explained the Scriptures like this to us. Our heavy hearts began to beat again. We quickened our step, wondering what all this could mean. Perhaps Jesus' death wasn't pointless after all. What if the kingdom Jesus had talked about hadn't come to an end? What if it was still alive in the hearts of his followers?

All too quickly we had reached Emmaus. I recognized the white roof of my house on the hillside. The stranger wrapped his cloak around him.

'Well, thank you for your company. I must leave you now.'

'Please don't go yet,' I said. 'It's getting late. Why don't you stay and have some supper with us?'

Our companion readily agreed and I led the way up the grassy slope to my house. Soon we were sitting down together for a simple meal of

bread, wine and figs. It was the custom for the host to ask God to bless the meal, so I was surprised when my visitor took the bread in his hand and did it himself.

'Father, thank you for this food,' he said.

As he spoke the words, his voice stirred something within me. I saw his face as if for the first time that day. And I found myself staring in wonder. Levi was staring too. The stranger's face, his voice... how could we not have recognized him before?

'Jesus! Master!' I exclaimed.

Levi jumped to his feet.

The next moment Jesus was gone from the room!

* * *

We never finished our meal. Under a milk-white, full moon, we set off—back along the road to Jerusalem. On the journey to Emmaus we had dragged our feet and talked in low voices. Now we walked with quick strides, chattering excitedly to each other. Wait till Peter and the others heard the news. The women had been telling the truth: Jesus *was* alive. The king had come back to claim his kingdom—and we had seen him ourselves. Now anything was possible!

THE ANIMALS' CHRISTMAS
& OTHER STORIES
Avril Rowlands

A donkey entered the stable. On his back was
a young girl. An older man followed on
foot...

'Humans?' spluttered the ox. 'Staying in
my stable? Well, I'm speechless!'

'Thank goodness for that,' said the goat.

On the first Christmas night events in the
stable in Bethlehem were far from ordinary.
Share the fun, joy and wonder of Christmas
in this original collection of animal stories.
Its twelve tales feature animals of all kinds—
sheep and snakes, cats and camels, dormice
and donkeys, and many more besides.

ISBN 0 7459 3699 7

THE HAFFERTEE STORIES
Janet and John Perkins

Haffertee is a soft-toy hamster. Ma Diamond
made him for her little girl, Yolanda (usually
known as Diamond Yo), when her real pet
hamster died.

These books tell the adventures of the
inquisitive, amusing and lovable Haffertee
Hamster. Each book is illustrated with line
drawings and contains ten short stories, ideal
for bedtime reading or reading aloud.

ISBN 0 7459 2067 5   *Haffertee Hamster*
ISBN 0 7459 2070 5   *Haffertee's First Christmas*
ISBN 0 7459 2072 1   *Haffertee's First Easter*

THE DRAGONS OF KILVE
Beth Webb

The unexpected arrival of the baby dragons—Horace, Maurice, Clarys, Sparky and Treasure—turns the peaceful life of the dragons of Kilve upside down. It leads to all sorts of adventures and mishaps: Igneous and Furnace get into a hot spot, Maurice's pride leads to a muddy fall, and Treasure lives up to her name.

Twelve funny and imaginative stories showing how everyone is special and the importance of caring for one another.

ISBN 0 7459 2747 5

All Lion books are available from
your local bookshop, or can be ordered
direct from Lion Publishing. For a free
catalogue, showing the complete list of
titles available, please contact:

Customer Services Department
Lion Publishing plc
Peter's Way
Sandy Lane West
Oxford OX4 5HG

Tel: (01865) 747550
Fax: (01865) 715152